I DON'T WANT TO KISS A ♥ LLAMA!

Written and illustrated by

Byron von Rosenberg

May your lips always be
long enough to kiss the
ones you love!
Byron

DEDICATED TO
YOU!

May you and your family enjoy the time
spent together with this book
making faces, laughing, hugging,
and (bleah!) kissing.
God bless you!

AND TO
ERIN VON ROSENBERG

who first uttered those immortal words:

"I don't want to kiss a llama!"

WITH SPECIAL THANKS TO

SHARON VON ROSENBERG
and
RYAN VON ROSENBERG

I don't want to
kiss a llama,
though they're cute
I must admit,

but when they pucker up
it's 'cause they're going to spit!

I don't want to
kiss a giraffe!

They stand much
too tall, you see.

I'd have to stand
   on tiptoes

just to kiss one
   on the knee!

Besides, its trunk gets in the way
and my lips aren't long enough!

I wouldn't kiss a penguin

on its orange-colored beak.

I'm afraid it might
take out an eye
when it pecked me
on the cheek!

BUT...

I would kiss a llama,

penguin,

or giraffe.

I'd even
kiss an
elephant...

if it
would
make
you
laugh!

Yes, I would give a kiss
to each animal at the zoo...

but I'd rather save them all

and give every one to **you!**

I Don't Want to Kiss a Llama! is my first children's book. I had written several llama poems (poems are just better with llamas in them) and my wife bought a large stuffed toy llama. One day I held it up to my daughter Erin and said, "Erin! Kiss the llama!" to which she replied with the words that are now title to this book. Both she and my son Ryan draw beautifully and my mother is an artist, so I decided to try to draw the pictures myself. I was (and still am) amazed at how many people love the pictures first before they read the poem. I think it's because they say, "I want to play!" I hope this book brings you much joy.

May your lips always be long enough to kiss the ones you love!

Byron von Rosenberg
Byrnes Mill, Missouri

LOOK FOR MORE BOOKS BY BYRON VON ROSENBERG!

Don't Feed the Seagulls
Climb the Red Mountain
Thinking Upside Down
Dale the Uniclyde
O Christmas Treed!
Stars to Chase

I Don't Want to Kiss a Llama
Copyright ©2004 Byron von Rosenberg
All rights reserved

Packaged by Pine Hill Graphics

Library of Congress Cataloging-in-Publication Data
(Provided by Cassidy Cataloguing Services, Inc.)

von Rosenberg, Byron.

  I don't want to kiss a llama! / written and illustrated by Byron von
Rosenberg. -- 1st. ed. -- High Ridge, MO : Red Mountain Creations,
2004

  p. ; cm.
  ISBN: 0-9759858-0-9

  1. Animals--Juvenile poetry. 2. Love--Juvenile poetry.
3. Emotions--Juvenile poetry. 4. [Stories in rhyme.]. I. Title.

PZ.R674 I36 2004
[E]--dc22   0409

Printed in South Korea.